HELLO, I'm THEA!

I'm *Geronimo Stilton*'s sister. As I'm sure you know from my brother's bestselling novels, I'm a special correspondent for *The Rodent's Gazette*, Mouse Island's most famous newspaper. Unlike my 'fraidy mouse brother, I absolutely adore traveling, having adventures, and meeting rodents from all around the world!

The adventure I want to tell you about begins at Mouseford Academy, the school I went to when I was a young mouseling. I had such a great experience there as a student that I came back to teach a journalism class.

When I returned as a grown mouse, I met five really special students: Colette, Nicky, Pamela, Paulina, and Violet. You could hardly imagine five more different mouselings, but they became great friends right away. And they liked me so much that they decided to name their group after me: the Thea Sisters! I was so touched by that, I decided to write about their adventures. So turn the page to read a fabumouse adventure about the

THEA SISTERS!

Name: Nicky
Nickname: Nic
Home: Australia
Secret ambition: Wants to be an ecologist.
Loves: Open spaces and nature.
Strengths: She is always in a good mood, as long as she's outdoors!
Weaknesses: She can't sit still!
Secret: Nicky is claustrophobic — she can't stand being in small, tight places.

nicky

Nicky

COLETTE

Name: Colette

Nickname: It's Colette, please. (She can't stand nicknames.)

Home: France

Secret ambition: Colette is very particular about her appearance. She wants to be a fashion writer.

Loves: The color pink.

Strengths: She's energetic and full of great ideas.

Weaknesses: She's always late!

Secret: To relax, there's nothing Colette likes more than a manicure and pedicure.

Colette

VIOLET

Name: Violet
Nickname: Vi
Home: China
Secret ambition: Wants to become a great violinist.
Loves: Books! She is a real intellectual, just like my brother, Geronimo.
Strengths: She's detail-oriented and always open to new things.
Weaknesses: She is a bit sensitive and can't stand being teased. And if she doesn't get enough sleep, she can be a real grouch!
Secret: She likes to unwind by listening to classical music and drinking green tea.

Violet

Name: Paulina
Nickname: Polly
Home: Peru
Secret ambition: Wants to be a scientist.
Loves: Traveling and meeting people from all over the world. She is also very close to her sister, Maria.
Strengths: Loves helping other rodents.
Weaknesses: She's shy and can be a bit clumsy.
Secret: She is a computer genius!

PAULINA

PAULINA

Name: Pamela
Nickname: Pam
Home: Tanzania

PAMELA

Secret ambition: Wants to become a sports journalist or a car mechanic.

Loves: Pizza, pizza, and more pizza! She'd eat pizza for breakfast if she could.

Strengths: She is a peacemaker. She can't stand arguments.

Weaknesses: She is very impulsive.

Secret: Give her a screwdriver and any mechanical problem will be solved!

Pamela

Geronimo Stilton

Thea Stilton
AND THE JOURNEY
TO THE LION'S DEN

Scholastic Inc.

No part of this publication may be reproduced, stored in a retrieval system, or transmitted in any form or by any means, electronic, mechanical, photocopying, recording, or otherwise, without written permission from the copyright holder. For information regarding permission, please contact: Atlantyca S.p.A., Via Leopardi 8, 20123 Milan, Italy; e-mail foreignrights@atlantyca.it, www.atlantyca.com.

ISBN 978-0-545-55627-9

Copyright © 2012 by Edizioni Piemme S.p.A., Corso Como 15, 20154 Milan, Italy.

International Rights © Atlantyca S.p.A.

English translation © 2013 by Atlantyca S.p.A.

GERONIMO STILTON and THEA STILTON names, characters, and related indicia are copyright, trademark, and exclusive license of Atlantyca S.p.A. All rights reserved. The moral right of the author has been asserted.

Based on an original idea by Elisabetta Dami.

www.geronimostilton.com

Published by Scholastic Inc., 557 Broadway, New York, NY 10012. SCHOLASTIC and associated logos are trademarks and/or registered trademarks of Scholastic Inc.

Stilton is the name of a famous English cheese. It is a registered trademark of the Stilton Cheese Makers' Association. For more information, go to www.stiltoncheese.com.

Text by Thea Stilton
Original title *Cinque amiche per un leone*
Cover by Giuseppe Facciotto
Illustrations by Barbara Pellizzari (design) and Daniele Verzini (color)
Graphics by Chiara Cebraro

Special thanks to Beth Dunfey
Translated by Emily Clement
Interior design by Kay Petronio

12 11 10 9 8 7 6 5 4 3 2 1   13 14 15 16 17 18/0

Printed in the U.S.A.   40
First printing, December 2013

A THRILLING PROJECT

It all started one CLEAR autumn morning. My old friend Octavius de Mousus, the headmaster of **MOUSEFORD ACADEMY**, had invited me back to teach a class — a seminar on documentary **photography**.*
Of course, I accepted at once. I love squeaking to students about my experiences! Plus, I'd get to see my dear friends the **THEA SISTERS**.

Oh, pardon me, I almost forgot to introduce myself! My name is **THEA STILTON**, and I am a special correspondent for *The Rodent's Gazette*, Mouse Island's biggest newspaper. Colette, Nicky, Pamela, Paulina, and Violet — the **THEA SISTERS** — were the star students of the last class I'd taught at Mouseford.

* Documentary photography shows daily life through pictures.

For this seminar's final exam, I assigned a **SPECIAL** project: a real photo essay! My students immediately started making plans for their **PROJECTS**.

"I'll photograph all the experiments at the ***science fair***!" Shen exclaimed.

"I'm going to cover the **athletic** championship tryouts," Craig said.

"We want to do our project on the fishermice of Whale Island," Elly and Tanya declared.

Ruby Flashyfur wanted to capture the drama backstage at a **FASHION SHOW**.

Only the Thea Sisters had yet to decide on something. *That was unusual!* I realized that the mouselets were squeaking ***busily*** among themselves.

"It's a pretty ambitious project," Paulina was saying. "I'm not sure the headmaster

will give us permission. . . ."

"Permission for **WHAT**?" I asked, more curious than a cat.

Nicky looked up at me eagerly. "To go to Africa on a PHOTO SAFARI!"

I smiled. As always, the mouselets had surprised me with their CREATIVITY.

"What a fabumouse idea!" I said. "I've got the perfect place for you: **MASAI MARA**, in Kenya."

"The nature reserve that's famouse for its lions?" Violet asked.

"That's the one! A dear **friend** of mine, Professor Chandler, is conducting a research project there. I'm sure he'd be happy to help you."

"Shake your tails, sisters, we're going to **Africa**!" cried Pam, springing to her paws faster than a gerbil on a wheel.

Violet was cautious as always. "First, we need to ask the headmaster for permission!"

"Then, we need to book our **Plane tickets**," Nicky added.

"Don't forget about packing our bags!" Colette finished.

I looked at the mouselets with pride. I was certain they would do a marvemouse job! Little did I know what an extraordinary **adventure** awaited them. . . .

Shake your tails, sisters!

AN EARLY ARRIVAL

It was early in the **morning** when the Thea Sisters landed in Nairobi, the capital of Kenya. They hailed a taxi that dropped them at the National Museum.

"Are we in the right place, sisters?" asked Pam, **looking** around.

Violet **YAWNED**. "Yes. Malik, Professor Chandler's assistant, gave us this address."

"This is the place, all right, but there's no sign of Malik," Colette said.

"No Malik, and nobody else, either!" Nicky laughed.

She was startled by a surprise **smack** on the head. "Yee-OUCH!" The culprit was one of Colette's pink sandals. "Coco, what are you up to?!" Nicky asked her **friend**.

Colette was rummaging through her enormouse suitcase. "It was here, I'm sure of it. . . . Ah, here we go!" she exclaimed triumphantly, pulling on a floppy sun hat. "Now I'm ready to face the African sunshine!"

"I can't believe we're really here!" Paulina murmured DREAMILY.

"While we wait, we could visit the museum —" Violet suggested.

HOOOOOOONK!

A **SHARP** car horn interrupted her. A **colorful** van had stopped on the side of the road. A group of noisy mouselings **HOPPED** out. "Hi, Paulina! Hi, Colette!" "Hi, Nicky! How was your **TRIP**?"

The Thea Sisters looked at one another in

CONFUSION. "Um . . . do we know you?" Pam asked.

One **MOUSELING** stepped forward. *"Not yet, but we already know everything about you!"*

EVERYONE ON BOARD!

A smiling ratlet scrambled out of the *matatu*.*
"Okay, let's give our new friends some room
to breathe!" he said, making a **PATH** between
the mouselings. Then he turned to the Thea
Sisters. "Welcome! I am Malik. Please excuse
the exuberant greeting. My brother, **JOMO**,
and his friends couldn't wait to meet you."

"And we are very happy to meet all of
you!" Nicky replied, putting out her paw.

"Professor Chandler told me a lot about
you. I'm honored to be your guide to the
Masai Mara reserve," Malik said.

"We can't wait to **CHECK IT OUT**!"
replied Paulina.

"Then let's **MOVE** those paws!" Jomo

---

* A *matatu* is a van with ten or more seats used for public
transport in Kenya.

exclaimed. The other mouselings **CHORUSED** their approval.

Malik laughed. "**LOOKS** like the mouselings have made the decision for us. Okay, welcome aboard!"

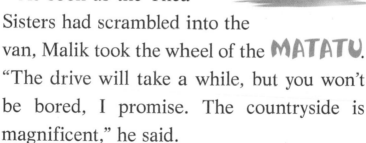

As soon as the Thea Sisters had scrambled into the van, Malik took the wheel of the **MATATU**. "The drive will take a while, but you won't be bored, I promise. The countryside is magnificent," he said.

"Plus, you've got us for **company**!" Jomo shouted.

"We can play games!" added one of his friends, **showing** them a soccer ball.

Malik glanced in the rearview **mirror**. "Can't you go a single day without playing?! No soccer inside the van!"

Jomo looked **glum**. "But we're a team. We can't abandon our soccer ball!"

"A team?" Nicky echoed, curious.

"Yes, we're the **Leopards**! We practice every day in Grandfather's field," Jomo explained.

"For now, you're just Leopard **cubs**," his older brother reminded him.

Jomo pouted. "This year, we beat everyone in the village tournament."

"I'm sure you're **wonderful**," said Colette, smiling. "We'd love to watch you play."

"Really?" **JOMO** replied, brightening. "Next time we'll invite you to **ROOT** for us!"

"We'll be there, we promise!" Nicky said.

"I don't know if you'll have the time, since you're going on **SAFARI**," said Malik. "I've prepared a **busy** schedule for you. It'll take a while to show you the wonders of the Mara."

"Speaking of **WONDERS**, look!" Paulina exclaimed, pointing to the countryside out the window.

The friends turned to **admire** the endless savanna on either side of the road. In the distance, they could see the outline of a jagged rock wall.

"We're in **Rift Valley**," Mailk explained. "Have you heard of it?"

"Of course!" Violet replied. "It's an **ENORMOUSE** valley created by the movement of the earth's crust."

"Violet is our walking, talking **encyclopedia**," Nicky said, grinning.

"It's no big deal — I just **LOVE** natural science," Violet said, blushing.

"**YUP**, and math, music, astronomy, literature, and just about every other topic I can think of! You're even an expert on **insects**," Colette joked.

Malik smiled. "You'll love Kenya, Violet. It's full of surprises! There's so much to learn here. As my grandfather says, *nature* always has something to teach us!"

Rift Valley

RIFT VALLEY is a large valley that extends for more than four thousand miles, from JORDAN to MOZAMBIQUE. The rift has been forming for more than thirty million years! It was created by the same movements of the earth's crust that separated the African and Asian continents.

THE RIFT VALLEY
in eastern Africa

KENYA

WELCOME!

Between the mouselings' lively chatter and the amazing scenery outside, the long hours of the trip **FLEW** past. It was already dark when Malik stopped the van.

"Here's our village!" he said as the mouselings **jumped** out of the *matatu*. "**JOMO** and I live with our grandfather in that house over there."

"Behind it is the **SOCCER** field where I train every day with my *friends*!" Jomo exclaimed, **SKIPPING** ahead. "Can I show you?"

Malik shook his snout. "Not today. It's late, and I

have to **DRIVE** the mouselets to the camp. Run home — we'll see you later." He started up the *matatu* again.

"Camp?! Are we going to sleep in a **tent**?" asked Colette, worried.

"What's wrong, Colette? Afraid there won't be room for all your **LUGGAGE**?" Pam teased.

"Actually, I was thinking of all the **bugs** that might be around. . . ." her friend replied nervously.

"Do you mean . . . there could be spiders?" Pam gulped, **ALARMED**.

Nicky shook her snout. "Mouselets, this is going to be more **fun** than a trip to CheeseFest! As long as we're careful, we won't run into any danger."

"Nicky's right." Malik nodded. "You'll be sleeping in fully **outfitted**, comfortable tents.

The camp is quite deluxe — there's even a small restaurant."

"Restaurant? Now we're cooking with cheese! In that case, I'm sure I can handle a few TİNY little spiders. . . ." said Pam, rubbing her belly.

Her friends laughed. Pam was notorious for her love of eating.

Meanwhile, the *matatu* had reached the GATES of the camp.

"We're close to one of **MASAI MARA'S** entrances," Malik explained. "Tomorrow, we'll begin the safari. You're going to have a great time!"

"I can't wait!" Nicky exclaimed happily.

"Me, either," Violet said, YAWNING. "But for now, let's get settled."

The Thea Sisters waved to Malik and arranged to meet early the next morning.

One of the camp guides helped carry their bags and took them to their lodgings: two TENTS furnished with comfortable beds covered with mosquito nets.

"I'm totally wiped out, mouselets!" Violet exclaimed. "I'll be asleep the second my snout hits the pillow."

Colette immediately started to unpack. Nicky, Pam, and Paulina decided to explore the camp with the guide. They wanted to take a look at the STARRY SKY.

"From those towers, there's a great view of the river Talek," the guide explained after a few minutes' walk. He gestured to an observation point. "Tomorrow morning, in the sunlight, you'll be able to see the whole countryside."

"We'll have to check it out," Paulina agreed. "What do you think, Pam? PAm?" She looked

around for her friend, who'd been next to her a moment before. "Where'd she go?"

Nicky *grinned* mischievously. "I'll give you one guess."

Paulina understood immediately. She turned back to the guide. "Could you please show us to the **restaurant**?"

Sure enough, Pam's stomach had led her to the restaurant. She was perched on a stool, sipping a **passion fruit** smoothie. A STEAMING plate sat in front of her. "These sweet potatoes are whisker-licking good!" she told her friends.

"Pam, you're hopeless!" Nicky and Paulina cried. But they couldn't resist, either. In no time, they'd joined her for a **SNACK**!

LET THE
ADVENTURE BEGIN!

The next morning, the sun had just **RISEN** above the horizon when the THEA SISTERS reached the entrance to the Masai Mara reserve.

There was no one waiting for them. Their **appointment** with Malik wasn't for another half hour.

"Didn't I say we were too early?" said Violet, **yawning** loudly. "You didn't let me sleep long enough, and we have a busy day ahead!" She was **CRANKIER** than a cat woken from a nap.

"We'll definitely be **busy** dealing with Vi's bad mood. . . ." Pam whispered in Paulina's ear.

"You can say that again, sis! If Violet doesn't get a good night's sleep, she's more **ferocious** than a cheetah!" Paulina replied, laughing.

"I heard that!" said Violet, shooting her friends a **GRUMPY** look. "And FYI, the **LEOPARD** is the most ferocious feline."

"That's true," a male squeaked from behind them. "But if you want my advice, you'd be wise to steer clear of both of them!"

"Malik! You're here," Nicky exclaimed, beaming. "We're ready for the safari!"

"Great, then let's *enter* the reserve. We'll take that **SUV** over there," the ratlet said, motioning. "This is Fadhili. He works with Professor Chandler and me at the Wildlife Center. He'll be our driver during the safari. Today he'll take us to an area of the Mara where we can **EXPLORE** by paw —"

A happy shriek from Pam interrupted him. "**MOLDY MOZZARELLA!** This isn't just any SUV, it's a rocket on four wheels!" She sighed in admiration. "What a thing of beauty. . . ."

Fadhili **MUTTERED** something in reply. As soon as they were all on board, he started the engine and took off.

"He's not much of a **SQUEAKER**, our driver. . . ." Colette commented.

"Fadhili is a bit of a loner, but he's an excellent ethologist* — and a great driver!" Malik said.

The **mouselets** didn't have time to answer, because as soon as the **VEHICLE** passed through the gates of the reserve, the breathtaking **COUNTRYSIDE** opened in front of their eyes.

"Welcome to the Mara. Let the **ADVENTURE** begin!" Malik exclaimed.

* An ethologist studies the behavior of animals.

Masai Mara

The great animal reserve Masai Mara is located in the southwestern part of Kenya. It is famous for its large prides of lions, but it is also home to many other species, including giraffes, elephants, zebras, rhinoceroses, and hippopotamuses. Masai Mara is part of the Serengeti ecosystem — a well-watered plains region that is an ideal habitat for the many animals that live there.

CLOSE ENCOUNTER!

The SUV soon reached the heart of the **SAVANNA**. Each of the Thea Sisters pulled out her camera.

"Ready, mouselets? We need to bring thousands of **PHOTOS** back to Mouseford for our report!" Nicky reminded her friends.

"**Holey cheese**, look over there! A giraffe!" shouted Pam, pointing to an elegant shape moving in the distance.

"And there are some **zebras** over there!" Paulina said. "Amazing!"

CLICK CLICK CLICK

As the mouselets snapped picture after picture, Malik commented, "Did you know that every zebra's coat is unique? It's impossible to find two with identical stripes!"

"Really? They all look the same to m —" But Paulina was interrupted by the **SUV** suddenly braking.

"We're here," Fadhili announced. "From this point on, we'll need to go on paw to see the WHITE RHINOCEROSES."

"The Masai guide will accompany us," Malik explained, introducing a ratlet who was waiting for the group. "We'll be safe with him!"

"But we must still be careful," Fadhili added. "It's best to stay close together."

The group walked behind the Masai guide, following a path that led toward a group of acacia trees. As they scurried along, they looked around with **WONDER**.

"Incredible . . ." Pam murmured. "Vi, will you pass me the **binoculars**? I want to take a closer look at some of these animals."

Violet passed the binoculars to her, and Pam began to study every corner of the savanna. "There's a pool of **water** over there, with beautiful birds around it. And look, sisters!" she exclaimed. "There's a **RHINOCEROS** right over there! That's funny, it seems to be staring at me. . . ."

"Um, actually, it *is* staring at you, Pam!" Violet said. "And it's not far away — it's **right in front of you**!"

"Wh-what?" Pam said, lowering the binoculars in **SURPRISE**. Sure enough, there was an enormouse white rhinoceros right smack in front of her. It was gazing at her CALMLY.

"You were looking through the binoculars backward. So instead of making faraway animals look **CLOSER**, it made close ones look **FARAWAY**!" Violet explained.

"Stay **CALM**," Malik suggested, inching toward her. "The white rhinoceroses that live here are used to visitors. Move carefully and it won't bother you."

"White rhinos may be **BIG**, but they aren't ferocious," Fadhili added.

"Pam, take a **picture**! This is the perfect chance for a **CLOSE-UP**!" Colette giggled.

"Er, that's okay," her friend said, backing away slowly. "Right now I'm more interested in keeping my **fur** in one piece!"

"We must **disturb** the animals as little as possible," Malik said solemnly. "This is their home, and we are just guests."

As they continued their hike, Malik shared the **secrets** of the reserve, and the mouselets

photographed each enchanting detail. Fadhili mostly remained silent.

"That mouse is definitcly quieter than your average rodent," Colette whispered to Nicky as they headed back to the SUV.

"You said it, sis," Nicky agreed.

Just then, Fadhili **squeaked** up. "Come on, let's get in. It's time!"

"Time for what? Back to camp already?" Colette asked, **surprised**.

"No, not yet!" Malik replied. "It's time to go meet the king of the Mara — his majesty, the **Lion**!"

White Rhinoceroses

White rhinoceroses are a very rare species. They like company and tend to gather in small groups called crashes. Their habitat is open plains, and they feed on grass. In spite of their name, their coloring is very similar to that of black rhinoceroses, their more solitary, aggressive cousins.

LITTLE MOSI

The **SUV** rumbled along a dirt path for a few minutes, then **SLOWED** to a stop.

"What's happening?" Paulina asked. "We've only gone – *ooooh!*"

Paulina's cry of amazement made her friends cluster around her. Just a few steps away, a beautiful lioness stood in the middle of the path.

"This is one of the queens of the area," Malik said. "As you know, the Mara is home to many lions."

"How exciting! I didn't think we would **SEE** one so close! But . . . how will we get past her?" Nicky asked.

Malik **shrugged**. "We'll wait for her to get up. We don't have much choice!"

Luckily, a few moments later, the lioness got to her **paws** and strode gracefully back to a pride of lions. The SUV continued along the dirt path and stopped not far from a STREAM.

"Look!" Malik said. "There's another pride of lions over there. If you LOOK closely, you'll see something very special. . . ."

The mouselets raised their binoculars and **gazed** at the spot Malik had pointed out.

"I see the lions, but . . . oh, oh!" Nicky EXCLAIMED in surprise. "It's a lion cub!"

"That's right," Malik said. "About two months ago, a lioness in this pride, who we named Lea, gave birth to this splendid LITTLE LION. We call him Mosi, which means 'firstborn.' Usually, three or four cubs are born at once, but MOSI was born all by himself, which means we have to take extra-special care of him."

"He's so adorable!" Paulina commented. "He's trying to stand up, but he's so shaky."

"He's been learning to walk, but his BALANCE isn't quite steady yet," Malik explained.

A moment later, a lioness walked up to the little one and rubbed his head with her nose. She licked him, and he fell *asleep* between her paws.

"Every day, Fadhili and I come here to monitor the pride and keep an eye on the lion cub. When you're a tiny lion cub, surviving on the SAVANNA is no piece of cheesecake!" said Malik.

"Malik is right. The savanna is full of **dangers**," Fadhili added. "That's why we

watch the **LION CUB** so closely."

"Go ahead and take your photos," Malik said. "Then we'll go back to camp. I have another *SURPRISE* in store for you!"

A SPECIAL EVENING

Malik's **SURPRISE** caught everyone off guard . . . everyone, that is, except Colette.

"I just knew an *evening gown* would come in handy!" she exclaimed, pulling a cloud of pink satin out of her suitcase.

"You don't think I can get away with a **SAFARI** outfit, do you?" Pam moaned, falling onto her bed. She hated dressing up.

"A gala evening on safari!" Colette sighed. "It's like a something out of a **FAIRY TALE**!"

"And did you hear what Malik said?" Nicky asked. "The gala's hosts are also the camp's owners, the Van Lupins. They're paying for the Wildlife Center's research on lions, so we've got to **dress to impress**!"

A little later, a squeak called out from the

tent's entrance. Nicky peeked out and found Malik waiting. He looked very *elegant*.

"Oh! You're — you look —" she stammered.

"Like a penguin?" Malik joked. "I know. I usually dress in comfortable CLOTHES, but sometimes it's not possible."

"I **know** just what you mean!" Nicky laughed.

Soon the **mouselets** were on board Malik's SUV, heading toward the Van Lupin MANSION. "**WHOA**, this place is swankier than soft **cheese**!" exclaimed Pam, scrambling out of the car.

The front door

opened, and a *snooty* butler greeted them. "Master Malik and mouselets, good evening. Please come in."

Colette scurried in first. Her **jaw** dropped at the **STATUES** and priceless **PAINTINGS** that adorned the walls. The entryway led to an immense ballroom **PACKED** with guests.

"**WOW**, this place is wild," Paulina murmured, looking around. "And not wild like the **SAVANNA**, either!"

Malik led them to the center of the party. "I want to **introduce** you all to someone. Ah, there he is."

In one corner of the room, a small group of guests were chatting. Malik approached one of them, a friendly looking gentlemouse who **gestured** broadly as he squeaked. "And when Mosi grows up nice and strong,

we'll have a new male lion who —"

"Professor Chandler?" the ratlet said **quietly**.

"— will be an important new member of the —"

"Professor Chandler," Malik repeated a little louder.

"— feline community of —"

"**PROFESSOR!**" Malik almost shouted.

"Hmm? Oh, it's you, my dear ratlet. And look who you brought with you! You must be the **FAMOUSE** Thea Sisters. It's a pleasure to meet you. I'm Harry Chandler."

"Thea's **friend**!" Paulina exclaimed. "Pleased to meet you."

"I've read all your **RESEARCH**," Violet said, putting out her paw.

"You're interested in **ethology**?" the professor asked her.

"Why, yes, among other things."

"Wonderful! Have you read my **latest** article in the *Journal of Science*? I reported on the data from a recent study. . . ."

"AHEM . . ." murmured the couple with whom the professor had been squeaking.

"Oh, how **rude** of me!" Professor Chandler exclaimed. "I haven't INTRODUCED you. Mouselets, these are the Van Lupins,

Pleased to meet you!

illustrious **art** collectors and **generous** patrons of our research! Sir, madam, may I present the Thea Sisters, five visiting students from **MOUSEFORD ACADEMY**. They are studying journalism."

"Aspiring **JOURNALISTS**? Interesting! As long as you don't ask too many questions, heh, heh, heh," said Mr. Van Lupin, stroking his **WHISKERS** nervously.

"I'm not sure what you mean. . . . We're here to create a **PHOTO** essay of life on the reserve," replied *nicky*, a bit confused.

"Oh, how nice! I am Ludmilla van Lupin. If you need

anything . . . but I'm sure that Malik will take good care of you! And now **PLEASE** excuse me, I see our friend the ambassador over there, and I must say **hello**! Come, darling," said Mrs. Van Lupin, dragging her husband with her.

"What strange rodents," Nicky commented. But before she could say anything more, Malik gently took her by the paw and invited her to dance.

NOT EXACTLY
AN EXPERT

While Nicky and Malik **twirled** across the dance floor, the other mouselets took a look around the mansion. It was truly amazing! The ballroom was connected to many other rooms, all **richly** furnished.

"This place makes me feel tinier than a newborn mouseling. It's so **huge**!" Pam said as they wandered around.

"You can squeak that again. It's pretty remarkable," Violet whispered in awe.

"Look at this **mirror**! Isn't it fabumouse?" Colette trilled. She peered at her reflection. "AAHHH! ROTTEN RATS' TEETH!"

"What's wrong?!" cried Pam.

"Why didn't anyone tell me that my fur is a

total fiasco?! It must be the warm Kenyan air," Colette squeaked.

Pam sighed with relief. "You mean you let out that cheese-curdling **SHRIEK** over the state of your fur-do? You **scared** me!"

Violet took her by the paw. "Forget it, Pam. You know that Colette's fur is her Achilles' paw! Let's go **LOOK** at the paintings back in the entryway."

Pam followed her friend to the mansion's entrance. As they admired the canvases, they could hear **ANXIOUS** voices squeaking. It sounded like an argument.

"There must be someone **BEHIND** that door. . . ." Pam said.

Curiosity drew the mouselets **CLOSER**, just in time to hear someone say, "This specimen will bring us a lot of money. You must find a way to get our paws on it!"

"It's Ludmilla van Lupin," Violet whispered. "I wonder what she's talking about!"

Just then, Pam **tripped** on the carpet and couldn't stifle her squeak of pain.

The door flew open, and Mrs. Van Lupin APPEARED. "What are you doing here? That is, um, my dear mouselets! Why aren't you dancing?"

"We were admiring your artwork," Violet replied. "The Andy Warmouse painting is **gorgeous**!"

"The Warmouse . . . oh, of course, this one." Mrs. Van Lupin indicated the canvas depicting a dancer.

"Actually, that's a Rattegas," Violet replied, **AMAZED**. "The Warmouse is that one there."

"Oh, of course! Excuse me, I must return to the PARTY. Come along." Mrs. Van Lupin led the mouselets back into the ballroom.

"Weird . . . for an art **collector**, Mrs. Van Lupin isn't much of an expert," Violet whispered.

"Want to hear SOMETHING even weirder?" Pam added. "I saw FaDHili in there with her."

"Fadhili? But why?" Violet wondered.

"I don't know. But I bet we can **find out**!" her friend concluded.

Actually, it's a Rattegas!

Ludmilla van Lupin is an art collector, but she doesn't recognize paintings by Warmouse or Rattegas — two very famous artists!

GO, JOMO, GO!

The next morning, Malik met the Thea Sisters back at the CAMP. "No safari today. Jomo needs you to cheer him on at his SOCCER match!"

By the time the mouselets reached the field, the Leopards were already warming up.

"You came! Hooray!" Jomo exclaimed. "Today we're PLAYING against the team from the next village over. They're very good!"

Hooray!

Malik ruffled Jomo's fur and addressed the team. "Give it your best shot, ratlings . . . and don't forget to have FUN!"

The Thea Sisters and Malik got settled on the sidelines.

Soon the game began. The Leopards played with lots of **ENTHUSIASM**, especially Jomo.

"Wow, Jomo's *faster* than the mouse who ran up the clock," Nicky commented.

Malik nodded. "He's always been full of energy. Grandfather says if Jomo raced a gazelle, he'd have a good chance of **WINNING!**"

Jomo drove the ball down the field past all his opponents, and took a shot at the goal.

"**Goal!** Hooray!" Malik shouted.

"Way to go, Jomo!" Pam yelled, jumping to her paws. "We should've made posters."

"Good job, little Leopard!" Malik shouted to his **BROTHER**, who shot him a huge smile.

"It's easy to see how much you **LOVE** him," Nicky said.

Malik nodded. "It's just Jomo, Grandfather, and me, and Jomo is still little. It's up to me to protect him."

"I have a LiττLe sister, and I feel the same way about her," Paulina said.

The game ended in a tie. Jomo was a bit **DISAPPOINTED**. He wanted to show his new friends that the Leopards were the best.

"Don't you remember what Grandfather said?" his older brother comforted him. "The important thing isn't the **number** of goals you score, it's the effort you put into the game."

"You Leopards sure put in a lot of effort. It was **SUPER-FUN** to watch you play!" Pam told Jomo.

"Squeaking of Grandfather, he's expecting us for a snack," Malik said. "**Mouselets, let's haul tail!** You're about to taste the finest cooking this side of the Serengeti!"

THE BIGGEST
DANGER

Malik and Jomo's house was very close to the soccer field. "I'm glad you'll get to meet my grandfather," Malik said. "He's a very **WISE** mouse."

The door opened, and a **PROUD-LOOKING** elderly rodent appeared on the doorstep. **"Welcome!** Our house is simple, but you must consider it your own." He invited the mouselets in and told them to make themselves comfortable around the table.

"It smells amazing!" Pam exclaimed.

"I've prepared one of my specialties: **COCONUT** rice and **banana** fritters," Grandfather replied. He served everyone a generous helping.

"Are you **HAPPY** to be here in Kenya?" Grandfather asked the mouselets.

"Yes, we're absolutely thrilled!" Colette replied.

"I just adore the **colors** and the **light** of Masai Mara," Paulina began.

"I'm very interested in African **culture** and traditions," Violet put in.

"I love the local **cuisine**!" added Pam, biting into a fritter.

"Pam, your **stomach** squeaks louder than your snout!" said Violet, laughing.

But Grandfather's reply was serious. "Even food expresses the character of a culture. There are many ways to nourish the body as well as the **spirit**."

"Well, what I like best is seeing Mosi the **Lion Cub**!" Colette said.

"Yes, Grandfather, he's growing strong,"

THE BIGGEST DANGER

Malik added. "Professor Chandler asked me to **MONITOR** him, so I check his 𝔭𝔯𝔬𝔤𝔯𝔢𝔰𝔰 every day. He is a little treasure for the reserve — we must keep him safe. There are so many **dangerous** animals on the savanna."

Grandfather looked at Malik *silently* for a moment. "I fear that the biggest **DANGER**

Kenyan Food

Kenyan cuisine is largely made up of vegetables, like SPINACH and CABBAGE, cooked with lots of spices. CORN is often used, sometimes on the cob, sometimes as cornmeal. The typical diet also includes, in smaller quantities, FISH, MEAT, and RICE.

for the little lion isn't other animals."

"What do you mean?" Nicky asked.

But Grandfather's only response was to shake his head **_mysteriously_**.

EVERYTHING ABOUT ELEPHANTS

The next morning, something unusual happened. Malik didn't meet the mouselets in front of the entrance to **MASAI MARA**.

The Thea Sisters waited for about half an hour. With every passing minute, they grew more anxious. "What's going on? Malik has never been a 𝕊ℙ𝕃𝕀𝕋 𝕊𝔼ℂ𝕆ℕ𝔻 late before!" cried Nicky.

"He must have been **DELAYED**, or maybe he forgot," Pam suggested.

"Forgot? No way! He couldn't have forgotten — he's our guide," Nicky objected.

Just then, the familiar **rumble** of Fadhili's SUV filled the air.

"There they are! Wait, it's just Malik. He's

alone!" Paulina said.

The ratlet pulled up in front of the tent. "Please **EXCUSE** the delay, mouselets. I waited for Fadhili at the Wildlife Center for a **LONG** time, and he just let me know he isn't feeling well."

"I'm sorry to hear that. I hope it's nothing **SERIOUS**," Violet said.

"He seemed fine yesterday," Nicky added.

"I don't think it's anything to worry about," Malik reassured them. "A little **rest** will get him back on his paws in no time."

The mouselets scrambled into the SUV, ready for a new day on **SAFARI**. Malik steered toward the river, to get a better view of the **HIPPOPOTAMUSES**. When he stopped the engine, the mouselets stuck their cameras out the windows.

"Try to be as quiet as mice. It's best not to

DiSTURB these hippos," Malik whispered.

"Why? They don't seem dangerous," Paulina replied.

"The hippopotamus has a reputation for being FEROCIOUS!" Malik replied. "Just like the crocodiles that live in these waters."

"LOOK over there!" exclaimed Pam, pointing toward the river. "Elephants!"

Malik moved the SUV closer so they could get a better look.

"There are even some little ones," Colette added. "THEY'RE SO CUTE!"

"Cute, yes, but not so Little," Violet observed. "A newborn elephant weighs more than two hundred pounds. Not exactly tiny!"

"They drink with their trunks, like gigantic straws!" said Paulina, peering at the elephants through binoculars.

"Actually," Violet said, "they use their trunks to suck up the **WATER**, and then they blow it into their mouths."

"Vi, you know **everything** about elephants!" Paulina said.

Violet laughed. "Well, not everything, but I was **READING** about them last night —"

She didn't get to finish her sentence, because just then an **elephant** used its trunk to **spray** dirty water right at the mouselets!

"HEE, HEE, HEE! Have you ever heard of an elephant shower, Violet?" Paulina said. "If you ask me, there are some things you

just can't learn from books!"

"To really **UNDERSTAND** something, I prefer to experience it up close and personal," Pam added, winking at her friends.

As the mouselets giggled, Malik looked off toward the **horizon**.

"Is everything okay?" Nicky asked.

"Yes, it's probably nothing. But I'm feeling something *different* in the air today. . . ."

"Really? It seems the same as **always** to me," said Nicky.

"Maybe we'd better go check on Mosi," suggested Malik. "I know I'll feel **better** after I see him."

Nicky nodded, and Malik revved the SUV's engine.

TRAPPED!

Malik grew even more worried when they reached the place where they'd SPOTTED Mosi the first day. The lion cub and his mother were nowhere to be seen!

"It's okay, they just moved. Let's take a look around and we'll find them," said Paulina.

But there was NO TRACE of the two animals anywhere nearby.

"They couldn't have gone far. **Where** could they be?" Malik was about to turn the SUV around when they heard a loud ROAR.

Mosi's mother, Lea, was a few yards away, striding around in a circle. As the mouselets and Malik drew closer, she let out another **ROAR**.

"Something's wrong," said Paulina. "I think Lea is trying to **tell** us something. . . ."

Malik pulled out his BINOCULARS to get a better look. The lioness was pacing around a deep hole. When he listened closely, he could hear a weak **moan** coming from inside. "Mosi must have fallen into that hole!" he cried in **shock**.

The Thea Sisters all started to squeak at once.

"HOW COULD THIS HAPPEN?"

"What's a **HOLE** doing in the middle of the savanna?"

"Something smells funnier than feta cheese. . . ."

"What if something **bad** happened to Mosi?"

Malik interrupted them. "We must let Professor Chandler know right away! He'll have the **EQUIPMENT** we need to get Mosi out. We'll take the cub to the Wildlife Center. I hope he's not hurt. . . ."

"Poor little guy . . ." Colette murmured.

Malik put the car in gear and hurried to the Wildlife Center.

"Do you think someone set a **trap** for him?" Nicky asked.

Malik shook a paw angrily. "Someone dug that hole on purpose. And it certainly wasn't another **animal**!"

"Your grandfather was right," Violet murmured. "But who could it have been?"

"Poachers try to capture animals from the reserve and **SELL** them," Malik replied sadly. "Someone must have lured Mosi away from the rest of his pride to **TRAP** him!"

Hello?!?

"How could someone do something so awful to a little lion cub?" Colette exclaimed indignantly.

"I'm calling the rescue team. We need to get Mosi to safety!" Malik said.

CARING FOR A BABY LION

The Wildlife Center's rescue team **rushed** to the preserve. They pulled **MOSI** to safety, and Zuri, the veterinarian, examined him immediately.

The cub had fractured one of his **legs** in the fall, and Professor Chandler decided to move him to the infirmary. Mosi would stay there until he had completely healed. The professor put Malik in charge of **WATCHING** over him.

"I'm not the right rodent for the job," Malik whispered, his snout down. "It was my **responsibility** to protect Mosi, and I failed. . . ."

"It's not your fault there are poachers, my

dear ratlet!" the professor burst out. "You did a great job!"

"But—"

"No buts. The lion cub will remain your **responsibility**," the professor declared.

The Thea Sisters tried to make Malik feel better. "We'll help you **take care** of him!"

"And so will I," said Fadhili, appearing at Malik's side.

And so will I!

"Are you feeling better?" Violet asked him.

"Yes, it was just a headache," said Fadhili. "Nothing too bad."

"What's important is that we're here to **HELP** Mosi," Malik said.

In the days that **followed**, Malik, Fadhili, and the mouselets took turns feeding and **watching** the little lion cub, who was kept in a large cage. Only Malik had the key. Professor Chandler checked his progress regularly.

"Poor little cub, he seems so sad. . . ." Colette said one morning.

"Mosi misses his mother and the savanna," Malik replied. "But the important thing is he's getting 𝔹𝔼𝕋𝕋𝔼ℝ. We should be able to free him in a few days."

"So soon?" Fadhili asked. "He still seems weak to me. . . ."

Malik shook his snout, smiling. "Mosi is STRONG, and his leg is healing. It's almost time for him to return to his kind!"

That same afternoon, it was Violet's turn to feed the lion cub. When she got to Mosi's room, she realized someone was already there.

"FADHILI?" she said. He was busy preparing the cub's food dish.

"Oh, there you are. . . . I saw that you weren't here, so I thought I'd take care of Mosi's food," Fadhili explained.

"But I'm pretty sure I'm not late!" Violet replied. She didn't understand why Fadhili wasn't sticking to the schedule. "Anyway, I'm here NOW, so you can go. Thanks."

Why was Fadhili preparing Mosi's food when it wasn't his turn?

An Evening of Surprises

That evening, a strange **wind** blew across the savanna.

"This wind gives me the **WILLIES**," said Colette as she and the other mouselets headed to Malik's for **DINNER**.

Pam laughed. "How can you have the willies when we've got Malik's grandfather's delicious dinner waiting for us? I've got to score a few of his RECIPES before we head back to Mouseford. . . ."

The Thea Sisters were greeted by a mouthwatering **aroma** the moment they walked in.

"Welcome!" Malik said.

The TABLE was covered with traditional

dishes. Grandfather invited the hungry mouselets to help themselves.

"This is super-tasty!" Pam said. "What is it?"

"*Ugali,*" Malik explained, "a dish made of **CORNMEAL**. You eat it with *sukuma wiki* — collards and kale."

Between bites, the friends discussed Mosi's accident.

"Some really **heartless** poachers must be after him," Malik said. "Usually, they attack elephants for their ivory tusks."

"Have poachers ever **ambushed** a lion here before?" Nicky asked.

"No, never. Professor Chandler and the **rangers** are forming a scout team to find their *HIDEOUT*."

"I'm not sure you're **following** the right strand of string cheese, my dear Malik," Grandfather said.

"What do you mean?" Malik asked.

Grandfather shrugged and said, "Perhaps the **CULPRIT** is someone closer to life on the reserve."

Malik began to ask Grandfather to explain when Jomo **BURST** into the room.

"Grandfather! Is it true?" the **RatLet** shouted.

"What's going on, Jomo?" asked Colette.

"I heard a **terrible** rumor. . . . Rodents are saying you want to **sell** our soccer field! Grandfather, say it's not so!"

"What? No way!"

Malik said. "That's CRAZIER than a cat chasing his own tail!"

"Not so crazy," his grandfather said. "The FiELD doesn't really belong to us."

"**WHAT?!**" Malik exclaimed.

Grandfather SIGHED. "The field used to belong to another family in the area. Many years ago, our family started taking care of the land. There were never any problems until a few months ago, when the new owners arrived. . . ."

"Who are the new owners? Maybe we could come to an agreement with them," Malik suggested.

"No, it's impossible. I'm afraid you've already met the new owners, and they are too stubborn! It's the Van Lupins."

AMBITIOUS PLANS

The next day, the **mouselets** and Jomo headed over to the soccer field.

"If the new owners build on the field, we'll need to **BREAK UP** the team. There isn't any other good place to play," Jomo said sadly.

"Maybe the Van Lupins will use the **LAND** to build an even better field," Pam said optimistically.

Just then, they spotted the Van Lupins at the field's **sidelines**. The couple was busy chattering with a **tall**, **THIN** rodent. Mr. Van Lupin had just unveiled the plans for an enormouse tourism complex.

As the mouselets drew closer, they heard him say, "We want this to be an **exclusive**, *elegant*, unique resort!"

His wife added, "Celebrities, movie stars, billionaires . . . Everyone will want to come here!"

"**HELLO!**" said Paulina.

Ludmilla van Lupin turned to greet them. "Ah, it's you, the **busymice** . . . I mean, those dear friends of Malik. What brings you here?"

An elegant resort!

"We're here to watch the Leopards, Jomo's **team**," Nicky explained. "It's their last game. They're very good. Are you a **SOCCER** fan?"

"I'm afraid I don't have the time. I have other, more **important** things on my mind," Mrs. Van Lupin replied, sticking her snout in the air.

"Ludmilla, my pet, we must choose the **MARBLE** for the grand staircase. What do you think? Rugged red or antique rose?" her husband asked.

"Sounds like you have **BIG** plans for this place," Nicky commented. "What are you planning to **build**?"

"Only the most exclusive resort in all of **KENYA**!" Mrs. Van Lupin replied proudly. "It will have every **LUXURY**: hot tubs, pools, a gym, and a huge golf course!"

"Come, dear, the architect is waiting," her husband said. "Excuse us, mouselets, but we have better things to worry about than **CHASING** a ball!"

The mouselets and Jomo headed onto the field. "Those two don't **care** at all about us or our team. I guess we better give up our dream of becoming GREAT SOCCER PLAYERS," Jomo sighed.

Hot tubs, pools, a gym . . .

"Don't ever give up on your dreams! You'll see, we'll find a way to fix things," Paulina said.

"That's right," Colette agreed. "We'll find a solution. For now, it's time to get on the field and give it your all!"

Don't ever give up on your dreams!

BABOON SNATCHERS!

After the game, the Thea Sisters went to the Wildlife Center to visit their little four-legged **friend**. They soon ran into Malik, who was beaming. "Mosi is almost completely healed! We might be able to set him **free** tomorrow morning."

"Hooray!" Nicky cried. "But . . . will we do it ourselves?"

Malik nodded. "Yes, but first we must **inspect** the savanna, to make sure that everything's okay and there aren't any new dangers. Let's go!"

As soon as the SUV entered the RESERVE, the mouselets realized how much they had missed it over the last few days.

"The **colors**, the LIGHT, the fresh

air, the animals . . ." Nicky sighed.

Malik smiled. "It's this place. It's just unforgettable."

"Hey, look — monkeys!" Paulina said, pointing to **shapes** swinging between the trees near the river.

"They're baboons!" said Violet. "Look, there's a mother with her Little one!"

"So adorable!" sighed Colette as she watched the baby baboon **HUG** its mother. "What cute animals! We've got to take some pictures. . . ."

After a while, Malik stopped at a picnic area. The mouselets enjoyed eating their snack outside in the fresh air.

As she bent over to pick up her canteen, Colette

heard someone behind her, pulling something out of her **backpack**. "Did someone take my cosmetics case?" she asked. "If you want to borrow my furbrush, just ask for it."

"Um, Coco, that might be a little **tricky** for them. . . ." Paulina said, pointing to a large baboon scampering away. He was clutching Colette's **pink** case between his paws!

"It's my fault — I should have warned you," Malik said. "Baboons tend to **snatch** whatever they can get their paws on. Was there anything valuable in your case?"

"Yes, something **EXTREMELY** valuable . . ." Colette murmured. "My anti-frizz kit for my fur!"

"Look on the **BRIGHT SIDE**, Colette," said Pam, trying to stifle a smile. "At least the baboons around here will have really

smooth fur!"

"We'd all better make sure we have everything we brought," Nicky suggested. "Okay, I'm not missing anything."

"Uh-oh — I am!" said Malik, his whiskers quivering with **worry**. "I can't find the key to Mosi's cage! But it couldn't have been the baboons. The key was in a pocket **inside** my backpack!"

missing!

The Thea Sisters surrounded Malik.

"Are you sure? Maybe the key just fell out of the pocket," Nicky said.

"No, I **LOOKED** everywhere in my backpack. . . ."

"Maybe you forgot them at the Wildlife Center," Violet suggested.

"I don't think so, but we'd better **go back** there and see!" Malik said.

Back at the Wildlife Center, a terrible **SURPRISE** was waiting for them. Mosi's **cage** was wide open and . . . **empty!**

"How — how

could this happen?!" Nicky spluttered. "Did someone **force** the lock?"

"No," said Pam, who was right next to the cage door. "It was opened with Malik's key!"

Malik ran to alert Professor Chandler, who joined them **immediately**.

"It's unheard-of! Who would steal a lion right out of my center?!" the professor cried.

"I only left him alone for a few hours. . . ." said Malik. He was down in the snout.

"I know, my dear ratlet," said Professor Chandler, giving him a pat on the tail. "I'll call the rangers. If this is the work of **POACHERS**, we must sound the alarm!"

Just then, Fadhili ran in. "I just heard about Mosi's disappearance! What a **cat-astrophe**!"

Professor Chandler turned to him. "You stay here and try to find out what happened. The mouselets will **HELP** you, right?"

The Thea Sisters nodded. The group split up: The professor returned to his office to call the police, Malik headed over to the **rangers'** station, and the mouselets found themselves alone with Fadhili.

"First things first," said Violet. "We need to find out what happened to **MOSI**."

"A poacher took him away, that's what happened!" Fadhili replied.

"Yes, but how?" Violet said. "I see a dish in his cage. Maybe there's some food left in it. It could be a **CLUE**. . . ."

"A food dish?" Pam said.

"Yes! Think about it — to move a lion, even a **small** one, you need to put it to sleep. And the fastest and safest way to do that is to put a tranquilizer in its food!"

"Of course!" Colette said,

picking up the food dish. "Let's take thiss to the lab for **analysis**."

"Give it to me, I'll take it!" said Fadhili, **grabbing** the dish out of her paws. "Wait here. I'll **see** you in a little bit."

"Hey!" Colette shouted.

"Don't mind him, Colette. He's just trying to help. He must be very worried about Mosi," Paulina said.

"**We all are**," Nicky agreed.

LET'S REVIEW THE SITUATION:

- Someone set a trap for Mosi.
- At the Wildlife Center, the lion cub was kept in a cage. Only Malik had the key.
- Malik, Fadhili, and the Thea Sisters were in charge of feeding Mosi.
- Someone took the key from Malik and stole Mosi.
- Did someone put a tranquilizer in Mosi's food? If so, who?

THE MYSTERIOUS SYMBOL

As they waited for Fadhili, Violet started to pace back and forth like a cat outside a mouse hole. "Let's **think** about this. Whoever kidnapped Mosi must have **stolen** the key to the cage from Malik. . . ."

"And so . . . ?" Paulina said, encouraging her friend to **continue**.

"And so . . . it couldn't have been a poacher. It had to have been someone who knew the lion cub was here. Someone who knows Malik . . ."

"**But who?** Wait, you don't think it's someone at the **WILDLIFE CENTER**, do you? They all seem like such **TRUSTWORTHY** rodents!" Colette exclaimed.

"I know. But it's the likeliest explanation," her friend replied. "Let's **LOOK** for clues!"

The mouselets started to **inspect** every corner of the room.

"There's nothing here," Pam concluded after twenty minutes of searching. "The thief didn't leave any clues. What do we do now?"

"It's time to move on to the next phase of the investigation," Violet declared. "We'll question everyone who knew what was happening with Mosi and try to reconstruct their **MOVEMENTS**."

"Good idea," Nicky said. "We'll talk with the vet who took care of Mosi. . . ."

"And we can ask the Center's biologist some **questions**," added Pam.

"We could also talk to the receptionists," Colette suggested. "If someone suspicious

ENTERED or **EXITED** the Center, they'd know about it."

The mouselets split up. Nicky and Violet headed over to see Zuri, but the **veterinarian** hadn't noticed anything unusual. "When Mosi disappeared, I was tending to a **BABY** antelope with my assistant, Masha."

Masha confirmed his story. "I was working in the infirmary, not **FAR** from **MOSI**. We didn't hear a thing!"

"Whoever took him acted quickly and **silently**," Violet deduced.

"Then they definitely must have used a **TRANQUILIZER**!" Nicky added. "Let's hope Fadhili discovers something."

Meanwhile, Colette and Paulina had gone to collect **information** from the **receptionists**. But . . .

"They didn't notice anything strange,"

Colette reported when she and Paulina returned.

"Are you **SURE**? Nothing out of the ordinary?" Violet asked.

"There was something!" a squeak behind them **EXCLAIMED**.

The Thea Sisters turned and saw a rodent in a **uniform** and a cap. He was the Center's janitor.

"I don't know if it has anything to do with

I found this!

the disappearance of the **LION CUB**, but I found this near the front door," he said, pawing a piece of **PAPER** to Nicky.

"'Gazelle,'" the mouselet read. "What does that mean?"

"It looks like a ticket to something," Violet replied, "but there's no address. Only the name and the **SHAPE** of a gazelle."

"Maybe the thief **dropped** it," Nicky said.

The mouselets showed the ticket to the receptionists, but they didn't recognize the **symbol**.

Discouraged, the Thea Sisters returned to the room where **MOSI** had been recovering.

"It seems like no one saw anything!" Nicky concluded. "The only possible clue is the picture of the **GAZELLE**."

Just then, Pam ran in. "Hey! The biologist is in Nairobi for a conference, so she can't

help us. Did you find anything?"

"Just a **TICKET** stub," said Paulina, pawing it to her friend.

"Hmm . . . I've seen this picture before," Pam said thoughtfully. "I'm **sure** of it! But I can't remember where. . . ."

A TRAP

The **SOUND** of pawsteps interrupted the mouselets' **CONVERSATION**.

"The analysis of Mosi's food won't be ready till tomorrow," said Fadhili, **entering** the room.

"Okay," said Paulina. She **pawed** the **TICKET STUB** to Fadhili. "The janitor found this, but we don't know what it means."

Fadhili took it. "I doubt that this has anything to do with Mosi's **disappearance**. Lots of tourists come to the Center. One of them must have dropped this during a *visit*. . . ."

"Hmm, there must have been a tourist visit today, then.

Interesting . . ." said Violet.

"What about you, Fadhili? Did you see anything?" asked Paulina. "Where were you when **MOSI** disappeared?"

"I was at the Van Lupins', taking away some **old furniture** they weren't using anymore. . . . I was thinking of bringing it to the Wildlife Center."

"So he has an **alibi**," Paulina whispered to Violet.

"**MOUSELETS**, we can't just stand around twirling our tails!" Colette said. "Time for the third phase of the **investigation**! Which is . . . uh . . ."

"We return to the savanna!" Nicky exclaimed. "Let's go back and check out Mosi's hole. Maybe we'll **FIND A CLUE** we missed earlier."

"Great idea, Nick! Mosi's fall and his

DISAPPEARANCE must be connected," Pam said.

Nicky turned toward Fadhili. "Can you drive us?"

"Sure!" the ratlet agreed. "*Let's go!*"

A few minutes later, Fadhili's SUV was heading for the heart of **MASAI MARA**. This time, the mouselets paid no attention to the wildlife. They were focused only on the search for clues.

When Fadhili turned off the engine, Nicky **immediately** recognized the place where they'd found Mosi. "Can we take a look around?"

"But . . . where's the hole? Won't we **fall** in?" Colette asked.

"Don't worry, I filled it in with **dirt** so no other animals would get hurt," Fadhili explained. He pointed to a spot where the grass was taller. "The **hole** was a few steps that way. If you want to explore, this is the time! I'll stand **GUARD** to make sure no animals come near."

The mouselets ventured over to check it out. But after a few **STEPS**, Nicky, Paulina, and Pam started to **SLIP**, and Colette and Violet soon followed them.

It took a few moments before they realized that they had fallen into the same hole as **MOSI**! Luckily, no one was hurt.

"What happened? Sisters, are you okay?" Nicky asked. "Fadhili, help! **We've fallen into the hole!**"

"*Fadhili! Fadhili!*" the others cried.

Only Violet didn't bother squeaking. "Mouselets, shouting won't get us anywhere. **He's the one who trapped us!**"

THE TRUTH

The other Thea Sisters **stared** at Violet in dismay.

"But — but how?" Paulina cried.

"He must've been the one who dug the **Hole** to capture Mosi, and who stole Malik's key!" Violet said.

"What about his **alibi**?" Pam asked.

"He made that up so we wouldn't suspect him," growled Nicky. The **TRUTH** had finally dawned on her.

"Congrats! You've figured it out at last," Fadhili snickered, peering into the hole.

"You kidnapped **MOSI**?!" Colette shouted.

"**Exactly!**" the ratlet replied. "It was easier than taking cheese from a mouseling."

"But everyone trusted you!" cried Colette.

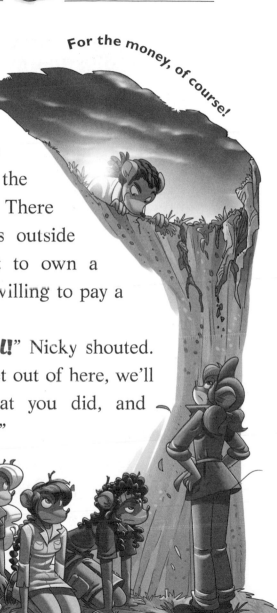

"**Why** did you do it?"

"**WHY?**"

Fadhili started to laugh again. "For the **MONEY**, of course! There are many rodents outside Africa who want to own a lion, and they're willing to pay a lot to get one."

"**That's illegal!**" Nicky shouted. "As soon as we get out of here, we'll tell everyone what you did, and you'll be arrested!"

For the money, of course!

"Sorry to **disappoint**," the ratlet replied sarcastically, "but it'll take hours for anyone to find you. By the time they do, I'll be on a private plane with your friend the **LiON cub**."

"Why, you sneaky, slimy sewer rat!" Pam spluttered.

There was no reply. Fadhili had `turned tail`, leaving the mouselets trapped!

"Oh no!" Pam **groaned**.

"I feel like I'm going to suffocate in here," moaned Nicky. She hated being in small spaces. "Maybe we can **call** for help."

"That'll just attract animals," said Violet, **shaking** her snout.

The friends all started to squeak at once.

"Animals? What do you mean?"

"Do you think we're in **danger**?"

"Bite your tongues, sisters!" cried Colette. "We're in trouble, it's true, but we can't panic! Malik will realize we've disappeared. He'll come **looking** for us."

"Good point," Pam agreed. "But maybe there's a faster way to get out of here. Nicky, you're good at **ROCK CLIMBING**. . . . Why don't you give it a shot?"

Nicky looked at the smooth walls of the hole. "It'll be tricky, but I can try!"

She gripped the **WALL** with all four paws. *Little by little,* she started to work her way up. She'd managed to get about halfway up when . . . **WHOOOOSH!**

A quick paw reached out and stole her cap. **"HUH?!"** Nicky was so astonished, she lost her balance and slid back into the hole. "Sorry, sisters, I can't do it. Plus, that baboon swiped my cap!" she sighed.

"It's becoming a habit!" Colette blurted. "First my cosmetics case, now your cap.

These monkeys are going to be so **stylish**!"

The Thea Sisters burst out laughing, **breaking** the tension.

But the **sunset** was starting to spread across the sky, and the mouselets were still **trapped** at the bottom of a hole in the middle of the savanna!

CHASING A CAP

Once he had alerted the rangers to Mosi's disappearance, Malik returned to the Wildlife Center. He had just entered the building when he realized that something **WASN'T RIGHT**: The room where he was supposed to **meet** the Thea Sisters was dark and silent.

"**MOUSELETS?**" he called.

No one answered.

"Fadhili? Is anyone here?"

NO REPLY.

"Where has **everyone** gone?" Malik murmured.

"Malik!" The sound of Jomo's squeal made his brother jump.

"Little brother, what are you doing here?"

"I heard that Mosi had disappeared, and I

wanted to help find him. But where are Colette, Nicky, Pam, Paulina, and Violet?" the little ratlet replied, looking around with confusion.

"I have no idea. . . ." Malik said, scratching his snout. "Maybe Fadhili took them back to their TENTS. Let's go see."

Soon the two brothers had reached the tents where the mouselets were staying, but they were empty.

"Let's try the **reserve**," Malik said thoughtfully. "It's Fadhili's turn to watch over the LION PRIDE tonight. Maybe he knows where we can find our friends."

Malik and Jomo climbed into the Wildlife Center's truck and hurried over to the reserve.

"I don't see Fadhili's *SUV*. . . ." Malik said.

"Look!" Jomo exclaimed, leaning out to

look at the **GROUND**. "Tire tracks!"

Malik climbed out to get a better look. The two brothers followed the tracks a few yards past the entrance to the reserve. Then Malik felt someone tugging the sleeve of his **SWEATER**.

"Jomo, wait. . . . I'm checking this out. . . ." the ratlet started. But when he turned, he was in for a **surprise**. It wasn't his little brother next to him, but a large baboon. In one paw, it held a green **CAP**, which Malik instantly recognized.

"Hey . . . that's Nicky's!" he exclaimed, trying to take it. But the **CRAFTY** monkey jumped away, then stopped and looked back at him **MISCHIEVOUSLY**.

While the baboon was focused on Malik,

Jomo leaped forward and stole back the **cap**. The **baboon** ran off scowling. "It's definitely Nicky's," Jomo said.

"That means that the mouselets are on the **SAVANNA**! We must go look for them." Malik raised his eyes toward the reserve, which was illuminated by the colorful **sunset**. "Soon, it will be completely dark. I'd better take you **HOME** first," he told his little brother.

But Jomo shook his snout stubbornly. "No, I want to go with you. The Thea Sisters are my **FRIENDS**, too. Besides, we don't have a moment to waste!"

Malik could see the determination in his brother's eyes. "Okay, let's go."

Malik steered the **SUV** into the Mara, and he and Jomo began searching the main road.

Suddenly, Jomo exclaimed, "Look, Malik!

That's Colette's **SCARF**!"

Malik slowed the SUV to a crawl. Colette's blue scarf **stood out** on the path in front of them. Jomo scrambled out and picked it up.

"They must be somewhere nearby. . . . Hey, we're in the area where Mosi got **hurt**!" Malik exclaimed. "Wait for me here, and **WATCH** for animals. I'll go look near the hole."

A moment later, Nicky heard a familiar squeak.

"Malik!" she exclaimed. "You came to rescue us!"

"**Mouselets**!
How did you get
DOWN there?"
called Malik as he
LEANED over the edge
of the hole.

"It's a long story. . . ." Violet replied. "We'll tell you **EVERYTHING** as soon as you get us out of here!"

Malik!

THERE'S NO TIME TO LOSE!

Once the mouselets were **SAFE AND SOUND** back in the SUV, they told Malik and Jomo everything they had DISCOVERED.

"Fadhili is the rat behind everything!" Nicky began. "He dug the hole so Mosi would fall in and **hurt** himself. Once Mosi was installed at the Wildlife Center, it would be

He dug a hole . . .   . . . then he stole the key . . .

easier to drug him."

"Then he **stole** the key to the cage, put a TRANQUILIZER in Mosi's food, and **KIDnaPPeD** him!" continued Violet, who had put it all together.

"And Fadhili trapped *us* by making us **FaLL** into the same hole!"

"Fadhili?! I thought he was my **friend**! I can't believe it. . . ." Malik said, stunned.

"Sorry, Malik," said Pam. "I'm afraid he's guiltier than a gopher in a gerbil burrow."

. . . and kidnapped Mosi!

"But why would he take **MOSI**?" Jomo asked.

"Some people think of animals only as **objects**," Colette replied.

"But that's terrible! We must save Mosi!" the little ratlet exclaimed.

"Yes, but **WE HAVE NO IDEA** how to do it," his brother said SADLY.

Nicky put a paw on his shoulder. "Yes, we do! Fadhili told us that he was taking Mosi on a private PLANE. Is there a runway nearby?"

"Yes, there's one not far from here, owned by the Van Lupins," Malik replied.

"Okay, then, let's shake a tail!" Violet said. "If we *HURRY*, I'm sure we'll find them there."

Fadhili is planning to use the Van Lupins' runway to take Mosi away. Whose private plane is he using?

FASTER THAN LIGHTNING

Twenty minutes later, the mouselets, Malik, and Jomo **sped** onto the Van Lupins' runway. Malik spotted Fadhili's **SUV** and stopped not far from it.

"Fadhili is here," the ratlet murmured, "and **MOSI** must be with him!"

Everyone scrambled out of the SUV. "Let's go!" exclaimed Jomo. He was ready to launch himself toward the **lights** of the runway.

"Stop, Jomo!" his brother said. "This could be very **dangerous**. You'd better stay here and wait for us."

"But I want to help Mosi! He needs me! I can't just stay here and watch!"

"No, Jomo! I can't let you —"

Violet interrupted the brothers' argument. "Malik, Jomo is right! To *free* Mosi, we need his help."

"But he's too little!" Malik protested. "I can't let anything happen to him!"

"**Don't worry**, he won't get hurt," Violet said. "All he has to do is **RUN**!"

"What do you have in mind, Vi?" Nicky asked.

"Who runs as quickly as a **gazelle**?" asked Colette, smiling. She had figured out Violet's plan.

"And who knows where Professor Chandler lives?" Violet said.

"I get it! You want me to run and alert the professor!" Jomo exclaimed.

"His house isn't **far**," Malik added. "And we could really use his help. Do you think you can complete this **MISSION**?"

Jomo straightened his tail with pride. "Of course! I'll run *FASTER* than a bolt of **lightning**. See you soon!"

As soon as Jomo was on his way, Malik and the mouselets turned their **EYES** back toward the runway.

"Now we just need to know which plane is carrying Mosi," Pam murmured.

"**LOOK!**" Violet exclaimed. "Do you see the **symbol** on that one over there?"

On the side of the first plane parked on the runway was the

outline of an antelope, along with the word
GAZELLE.

"The MYSTERIOUS symbol! It
really is connected to Mosi's disappearance!"
Nicky said.

"And that's not all," Violet added. **"Look
who's here!"**

STOP!

The Thea Sisters immediately recognized **two figures** next to the plane's entrance.

"It's the Van Lupins!" Pam said.

"The Van Lupins?!" Malik exclaimed. "But how is that possible?"

"That's where I'd seen the **GAZELLE** symbol before — on the plans for their resort!" Pam realized.

"I can't believe it!" Violet said angrily. "Of course, they weren't very convincing as **art collectors.** But I didn't think that they could actually be **trafficking animals!**"

"And there's Fadhili," said Paulina. "He's stowing those boxes on the **PLANE**. . . . Mosi must be inside! They're going to take him away!"

"Not if I have anything to squeak about it!" Malik exclaimed resolutely. "I'll do whatever it takes to stop them!"

"We'll **help** you," Nicky said, taking Malik by the paw. "Right, **mouselets**?"

"Right!" cried Pam.

"Friends together, mice forever!" said Paulina.

Malik and the mouselets **TALKED** for a few minutes, trying to decide what to do next. Then Nicky started dashing toward the runway.

"Stop!" she cried, running toward Fadhili and the Van Lupins. **"STOP!"**

The couple turned around, **surprised**.

"Wh-what are you doing here?!" Mr. Van Lupin exclaimed.

"Come to throw **mold** all over our cheesecake?" muttered Mrs. Van Lupin, rolling her eyes.

"I know about **everything** you've done, and I'm not going to let you leave with little Mosi!" Nicky **cried**.

"And just how do you propose to stop us, young mouselet?" Mrs. Van Lupin replied.

"I'll . . . I'll **get you**! My friends are alerting Professor Chandler as we **squeak**. We **won't** let you leave!"

Mrs. Van Lupin turned to her accomplice. "Fadhili, you're such a cheesebrain! Didn't you tell me that these **mouselets** were trapped like lab rats?"

"But I — that is — I was **SURE** that —" Fadhili stammered. He couldn't believe the mouselets had escaped.

"You're more useless than a bat in broad daylight!" Mrs. Van Lupin cried. Then, looking Nicky right in the **EYE**, she added, "No one can get in the way of our plan, least of all five **nosy** mouselets!"

"Well said, my pet!" her husband replied. "And, of course, the **LION** is already safe in the hold. . . ."

"**Shut your snout**, Edgar!" his wife interrupted. "Start the engine: We've already waited too long!"

But Colette, Pam, Paulina, and Violet had wasted no time. While Nicky **distracted** the Van Lupins and Fadhili, they had slipped on board the **plane**!

REINFORCEMENTS
ARE HERE!

Malik was lying in wait for the Van Lupins. As they climbed up the plane's stairs, he tossed a net he'd taken from the **VAN** and captured Edgar, Ludmilla, and Fadhili in one fell swoop.

"We've **CAUGHT** three predators more dangerous than wild animals!" Nicky exclaimed, satisfied.

"Edgar, **DO SOMETHING!**" Ludmilla squealed. Her husband clumsily tried to free himself, but he just tangled himself **tighter** than a mouse in a trap.

"This is completely **RIDICULOUS!** We must leave immediately and take our **LION** with us!" he cried.

"You're not going anywhere!" A **forceful** squeak interrupted them. "We're stopping you!"

It was Professor Chandler and a group of rangers. They had the Van Lupins completely SURROUNDED.

"You? But how . . . ?" Mr. Van Lupin's speech **faltered**.

A small, *speedy* figure stepped forward.

"Jomo!" Malik exclaimed. "You did it!"

"Yes!" the ratlet replied proudly. "I ran as *fast* as my paws could take me!"

"It's true," Professor Chandler confirmed. "When Jomo arrived at my house, he was out

of breath, but he managed to tell me what had happened. I alerted the **rangers**, and we ran to help you. But I see that you've done **very well** without us!"

While the rangers pawcuffed Fadhili and the Van Lupins, Nicky, Professor Chandler, and Malik headed over to the plane's **CARGO** hold. Inside, there were many **boxes** of different sizes . . . and four mouselets looking for a **little lion CUB**!

Pam had just located a large box with small **holes** on the sides. When the professor opened it, he recognized a familiar shape: At the bottom was little **MOSI**, fast asleep.

"W-we can explain everything. . . . It — it's not what it seems. . . ." the Van Lupins **stammered**.

"Of course you'll explain everything . . . in front of a ***judge***!" the professor replied.

"Trafficking animals is a very serious crime. You've **endangered** this lion cub just to make a quick buck!"

The rangers carefully transported the **box** to their SUV. A moment later, they were on the way back to the Wildlife Center.

"Now we'll **CHECK** the other boxes," the professor said. "I hope there aren't any more defenseless animals in here."

ANOTHER SURPRISE

With great care, Malik opened a SMALL wooden box. What he saw inside left him squeakless.

"A PAINTING!" he exclaimed.

"Here's another one. . . ." said Nicky, who had opened the top of another box.

"Um . . . they're . . . paintings from our collection, right, Edgar?" Ludmilla explained, grabbing her husband's paw.

"What are you squeaking — Oh! Of course! We just bought them!" he replied with a nervous smile.

Professor Chandler was suspicious. "Paintings? Hmm . . . let me see."

As soon as the professor saw the canvases, he let out a SHOUT. "Ah! I recognize these paintings!" he exclaimed, turning to the Van Lupins. "You most certainly didn't **BUY** these! Kidnapping a lion cub is just the tip of the cheese slice for you two. You've been **STEALING** precious works of art!"

"**Stealing art?!**" asked Malik. "Professor, what's going on?"

"These are two VERY VALUABLE canvases by the great Ulubu, the most famous painter in all of KENYA," Professor Chandler explained. He SHOWED the mouselets the canvases. "This one is called *Giraffes at Sunset,* and the other is the *famous Tired Lion in the Shade of the Acacia*!"

Pam studied the PAINTINGS carefully, looking from the RIGHT to the LEFT. "What lovely artworks!" she murmured.

"A dear friend of mine,

Professor Layton, acquired them long ago, and **HUNG** them in his home," the professor continued. "A few weeks ago, they were mysteriously stolen."

"And now you've **FOUND** them," Paulina said. "Looks like the Van Lupins were swiping whatever they could get their paws on."

"Well, they certainly aren't **experts** on fine art!" Violet burst out.

"Now **YOU** can return the paintings to their rightful **OWNER**," Paulina said.

"**No**," the professor replied, leaving everyone squeakless. "You mouselets should return them — and

COLLECT the reward!"

The Thea Sisters exchanged a look of surprise. "Reward?!"

"Yes, Professor Layton established a **REWARD** for whoever returns his paintings. And it belongs to you!"

"But . . . we can't . . ." Nicky faltered.

"**We can and we must!**" Colette exclaimed suddenly, pulling her **FRIENDS** close. "Mouselets, I have the most **FABUMOUSE** idea for what to do with the reward. . . ."

UNITED FOR VICTORY!

The sun was already high in the **SKY** when the Thea Sisters joined Malik on the sidelines of the soccer field. It had been a few days since they'd **freed** Mosi, and he was now safely back at the Wildlife Center.

Malik was **happy** and **relaxed**. "Mouselets, I can't thank you enough for all you've done," he told his **friends** as they sat next to him. "Using the reward for the paintings to get back the soccer field was just **marvemouse!**"

"Now no one can take it away from Jomo and his friends!" said Nicky, **smiling** as the Leopards **LEAPED** and bounced onto the field.

"I don't mean to brag, but those new uniforms are **TRÈS CHIC**!" Colette said.

With the reward money from the stolen paintings, the Thea Sisters had purchased the soccer field. As a bonus, they'd **given** the team new goals and balls. Plus, Colette had designed new **UNIFORMS** with the name of each player printed on the back.

"They really look like **leopard cubs**!" Paulina exclaimed.

"Hey, look who's coming to join us!" Colette said.

Malik's **grandfather** had just arrived on the field, along with Professor Chandler.

"I would never miss the first game on the field now that it's ours **AGAIN**!" Grandfather said.

"Me, neither. Especially since it's our **LAST CHANCE** to see Jomo play. I can't believe we have to leave tomorrow!" Violet replied sadly.

"That's a real **SHAME**," Professor Chandler said. "But . . . aren't we missing someone? Your friend with the **curls**?"

"Pam? She's coming. . . . There she is!"

Pam was scurrying toward her friends. She had a big **PACKAGE** in her paws.

"Hey, what's that?" Colette asked.

"Sisters! I couldn't come unprepared like last time," Pam explained.

Without another word, she opened the package and pulled out a **beautiful** banner.

GO LEOPARDS!

"It's the least we can do for our favorite **RUNNER**, right?" Pam said, winking at her **FRIENDS**.

"Right!" Nicky laughed. "Get ready to use your outside squeaks, mouselets! We've got some **CHEERING** to do."

GOOD-BYE, MOSI!

After Jomo's **GAME**, the Thea Sisters had just one more important job to do: bring little **MOSI** home to the **SAVANNA**. He was completely recovered at last!

Malik drove the mouselets to the reserve one last time. **GRANDFATHER** came along, too. He wanted to help set the *lion cub* free.

"At last Mosi will go home," Nicky said happily as they pulled up to the area where the lion had first fallen into the poachers' **TRAP**.

"Who knows if he'll remember us. . . ." Colette whispered as the little cub, finally free, placed a tentative paw on the **SAVANNA**.

As if he understood, Mosi turned his ***intense golden eyes*** to the mouselets,

who were watching him from the van. Then they heard a roar fill the **AIR**.

"It's Lea!" Paulina said. "His mother knows he's here!"

UNCERTAIN at first, and then more confidently, Mosi **TROTTED** away. Soon

he had disappeared into the undergrowth, where his **MOTHER** was waiting for him.

In the van, everyone was silent.

"This has been an **incredible** experience," Nicky said after a few moments. "Not just because we saw amazing PLACES, but also

because we were able to do something GOOD for Jomo . . . and to give Mosi back his freedom!"

Grandfather **LOOKED** at each of the mouselets fondly. "All that you've done for us is a great gift. Remember: The good that you do will return to you many times over!"

"JUMPING GERBILS!" Pam exclaimed, wiping her eyes. "I'll miss your grandfather, Malik!"

"And I'll miss you," Grandfather replied with a smile. "But I'm sure you already know that true friends stay in your **heart** forever!"

A REPORT FROM
THE HEART

When the Thea Sisters returned to Mouseford, they immediately got to work on their photo essay. Each mouselet focused on a different aspect of the project: Paulina laid out the PHOTOGRAPHS, Violet wrote the captions, Colette suggested colors and placement, and Pam took care of the projector.

Finally, Nicky gave it a few last touches, adding details taken from their travel DIARIES. She got a little help from Malik — the two friends were emailing each other almost every day.

When they presented their essay at my seminar, the report was complete in every way.

All my students did a great job, but the

THEA SISTERS' report had something special: Every page glowed with their *love* for the places, animals, and rodents they had photographed.

At the end of their presentation, I said, "Mouselets, you each earned an A-plus, because this report comes straight **from the heart!**"

THEY WERE MORE THAN FRIENDS. THEY WERE SISTERS!

Thea Sisters

Don't miss these exciting Thea Sisters adventures!

Thea Stilton and the Dragon's Code

Thea Stilton and the Mountain of Fire

Thea Stilton and the Ghost of the Shipwre

Thea Stilton and the Secret City

Thea Stilton and the Mystery in Paris

Thea Stilton and the Cherry Blossom Adventure

Thea Stilton and the Star Castaways

Thea Stilton: Big Tro in the Big Apple

Thea Stilton and the Ice Treasure

Thea Stilton and the Secret of the Old Castle

Thea Stilton and the Blue Scarab Hunt

Thea Stilton and the Prince's Emerald

Thea Stilton and the My on the Orient Expre

Thea Stilton and the Dancing Shadows

Thea Stilton and the Legend of the Fire Flowers

Thea Stilton and the Spanish Dance Mission

Thea Stilton and the Journey to the Lion's Den

Be sure to read all of our magical special edition adventures!

THE KINGDOM OF FANTASY

THE QUEST FOR PARADISE: THE RETURN TO THE KINGDOM OF FANTASY

THE AMAZING VOYAGE: THE THIRD ADVENTURE IN THE KINGDOM OF FANTASY

THE DRAGON PROPHECY: THE FOURTH ADVENTURE IN THE KINGDOM OF FANTASY

THE VOLCANO OF FIRE: THE FIFTH ADVENTURE IN THE KINGDOM OF FANTASY

THEA STILTON: THE JOURNEY TO ATLANTIS

THEA STILTON: THE SECRET OF THE FAIRIES

Don't miss any of my other fabumouse adventures!

#1 Lost Treasure of the Emerald Eye

#2 The Curse of the Cheese Pyramid

#3 Cat and Mouse in a Haunted House

#4 I'm Too Fond of My Fur!

#5 Four Mice Deep in the Jungle

#6 Paws Off, Cheddarface!

#7 Red Pizzas for a Blue Count

#8 Attack of the Bandit Cats

#9 A Fabumouse Vacation for Geronimo

#10 All Because of a Cup of Coffee

#11 It's Halloween, You 'Fraidy Mouse!

#12 Merry Christmas, Geronimo!

#13 The Phantom of the Subway

#14 The Temple of the Ruby of Fire

#15 The Mona Mousa Code

#16 A Cheese-Colored Camper

#17 Watch Your Whiskers, Stilton!

#18 Shipwreck on the Pirate Islands

#19 My Name Is Stilton, Geronimo Stilton

#20 Surf's Up, Geronimo!

#21 The Wild, Wild West

#22 The Secret of Cacklefur Castle

A Christmas Tale

#23 Valentine's Day Disaster

#24 Field Trip to Niagara Falls

#25 The Search for Sunken Treasure

#26 The Mummy with No Name

#27 The Christmas Toy Factory

#28 Wedding Crasher

#29 Down and Out Down Under

#30 The Mouse Island Marathon

#31 The Mysterious Cheese Thief

Christmas Catastrophe

#32 Valley of the Giant Skeletons

#33 Geronimo and the Gold Medal Mystery

#34 Geronimo Stilton, Secret Agent

#35 A Very Merry Christmas

#36 Geronimo's Valentine

#37 The Race Across America

#38 A Fabumouse School Adventure

#39 Singing Sensation

#40 The Karate Mouse

#41 Mighty Mount Kilimanjaro

#42 The Peculiar Pumpkin Thief

#43 I'm Not a Supermouse!

#44 The Giant Diamond Robbery

#45 Save the White Whale!

#46 The Haunted Castle

#47 Run for the Hills, Geronimo!

#48 The Mystery in Venice

#49 The Way of the Samurai

#50 This Hotel Is Haunted

#51 The Enormouse Pearl Heist

#52 Mouse in Space!

#53 Rumble in the Jungle

#54 Get into Gear, Stilton!

#55 The Golden Statue Plot

#56 Flight of the Red Bandit

Special Edition

The Hunt for the Golden Book

Join me and my friends on a journey through time in this very special edition!

Geronimo Stilton

THE **JOURNEY THROUGH TIME**

SCHOLASTIC

THE JOURNEY
THROUGH TIME

Meet
GERONIMO STILTONOOT

He is a cavemouse—Geronimo Stilton's ancient ancestor! He runs the stone newspaper in the prehistoric village of Old Mouse City. From dealing with dinosaurs to dodging meteorites, his life in the Stone Age is full of adventure!

#1 The Stone of Fire

#2 Watch Your Tail!

#3 Help, I'm in Hot Lava!

#4 The Fast and the Frozen

Meet
CREEPELLA VON CACKLEFUR

I, *Geronimo Stilton*, have a lot of mouse friends, but none as **spooky** as my friend CREEPELLA VON CACKLEFUR! She is an enchanting and MYSTERIOUS mouse with a pet bat named Bitewing. YIKES! I'm a real 'fraidy mouse, but even I think CREEPELLA and her family are AWFULLY fascinating. I can't wait for you to read all about CREEPELLA in these a-mouse-ly funny and **spectacularly spooky** tales!

#1 THE THIRTEEN GHOSTS

#2 MEET ME IN HORRORWOOD

#3 GHOST PIRATE TREASURE

#4 RETURN OF THE VAMPIRE

#5 FRIGHT NIGHT

THANKS FOR READING,
AND GOOD-BYE UNTIL OUR
NEXT ADVENTURE!

Thea Sisters